Griffin, Michael
    Salaama in Kenya. – (Beans)
    1. Kenya – Social life and customs –
    1963- – Juvenile literature
    I. Title   II. Liba Taylor
    967.6'204   DT433.54

    ISBN 0–7136–2852–9

A & C Black (Publishers) Limited
35 Bedford Row, London WC1R 4JH

© 1987 A & C Black (Publishers) Limited

Acknowledgements
The map is by Tony Garrett

Filmset by August Filmsetting, Haydock, St Helens
Printed in Hong Kong by Dai Nippon Printing Co. Ltd

Salaama in Kenya

Michael Griffin

Photographs by Liba Taylor

A & C Black · London

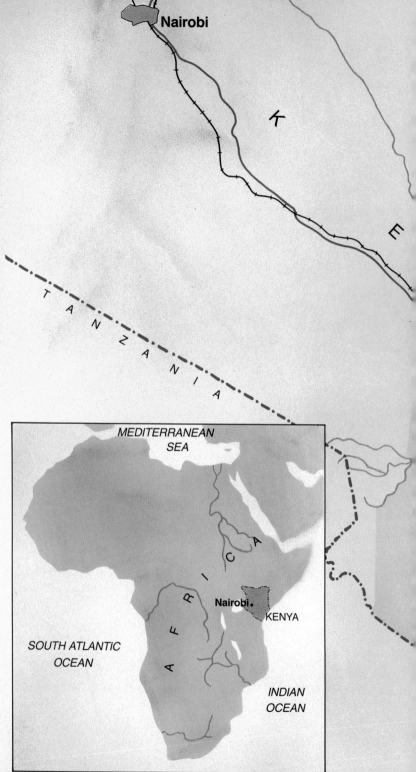

Nairobi

K

E

TANZANIA

MEDITERRANEAN SEA

AFRICA

Nairobi. KENYA

SOUTH ATLANTIC OCEAN

INDIAN OCEAN

My name is Salaama, which is the Kenyan word for 'peace'. I am ten years old and I have two younger brothers and a new baby sister.

We live near the city of Mombasa, because my dad, Hilary Katama, works there and my brother Philip and I both go to school nearby. My mum, Florence, looks after our farm in the country, but we all meet up in the holidays.

Mombasa is on the east coast of Africa and it's the second biggest city in Kenya. We live in a suburb called Magogoni. Though it's near the city, Magogoni is very quiet – more like a village really. It's surrounded by coconut trees and lots of people keep goats and chickens.

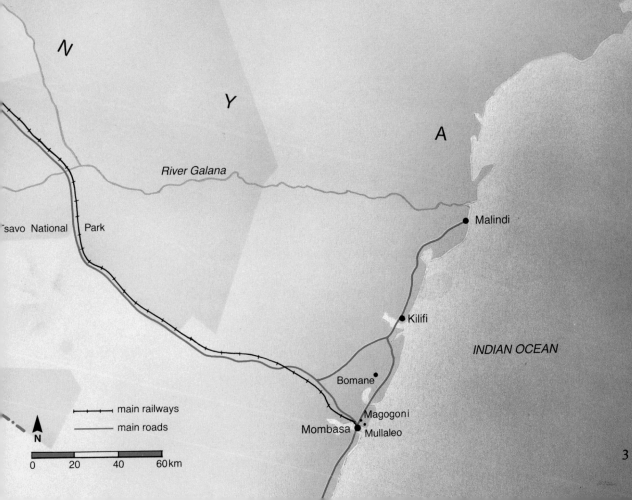

N

Y

A

River Galana

Tsavo National Park

Malindi

Kilifi

INDIAN OCEAN

Bomane

Magogoni

Mombasa   Mullaleo

main railways

main roads

N

0   20   40   60km

I'm not at school at the moment because it's the middle of our Christmas holidays. I've still got my hands full though, because Mum has brought the two youngest children down from the farm to spend the holidays with us.

I am holding my brother Christopher in one arm and baby Rita in the other. Christopher is only two years old but he's always getting into trouble. Rita is seven months old so she's still very light to carry. I am the oldest girl in our family and it's my job to take care of the house when Mum's not here.

One of my jobs is to wash our clothes. Look at that big pile I've still got to finish. That's our house, behind me. My dad built the house before I was born. It's made from cement blocks, which cost quite a bit but last for ages.

Lots of our neighbours live in houses made of mud and wooden poles, which are cheap but often need repairing. Our roof is made from coconut palms, which keep the rooms inside nice and cool.

We sometimes use the room with the big blue doors as a shop. We sell cooking oil, washing powder, tea and sugar – the sort of things that people need to buy every day. At the moment Dad is renting the room to a school teacher.

Like most of our neighbours, Dad has to get up
very early to go to work in Mombasa. He has a
twenty minute walk to the bus stop, which is near
our school in a place called Mullaleo. Dad catches
a matatu, which is a small white bus. It's different
from an ordinary bus because the driver will stop
and let you out wherever you want. He tries to
squeeze in as many passengers as possible so
it's a real squash inside.

In the holidays, we get up about an hour after Dad, and eat our breakfast in the yard. We have slices of bread and jam, with cups of sweet tea.

After breakfast, Charo the waterseller comes round to the house. Some people fetch their water in buckets from the public taps, but there is always a long queue, so we buy our water from Charo. We need to buy eight tins of water every day for washing clothes, taking baths and cooking. We pay seventy cents for every tin and then store the water in a big, blue drum.

Charo has lots of customers and all day he pushes the barrow around Magogoni. You can always tell when he's coming because the wheels of his barrow make a loud, jingling noise when they turn.

This is our local shop. It's just down the road
from our house. There's also a vegetable market,
a butcher and a little snack-bar nearby. People
in Magogoni don't usually go into Mombasa
unless they want to buy something special,
like new clothes.

When we have our own shop, of course, we hardly
need to go out at all! Now I always seem to be
popping out, so Peter the shop-keeper knows me
quite well. Outside Peter's shop, there's a man who
washes and irons clothes. I take our laundry to him
for ironing because we don't have an iron at home.

The butcher's shop is next door. Mum's a bit late today so there's not much meat left to choose from. She points at the piece she wants and asks the butcher to weigh it on his big scales. One of our neighbour's children has come to help her carry the shopping so I can go out and play.

My best friends are Suabaha and Mariam who are sisters. We live next door to each other but we go to different schools. Whenever we can, we all go out and play piggy-in-the-middle. Next to the house there's a big open space where we usually play.

In April, when the wet season starts, it will rain every day for weeks. Then people suddenly realize their roofs need mending, so they come to Mum to buy roof tiles. Mum makes the tiles out of palm leaves from coconut trees. We help her by collecting the leaves when they fall to the ground.

Every time a leaf falls from a tree, it makes a loud crashing noise. We all rush out and see who can get it first. Philip won this time and he's pulling off the stalks for Mum to use.

Palm leaves are very tough. Even Philip, who is quite strong, has to struggle to pull off the stalks. Christopher didn't win the race, but he did find two coconuts!

Mum can make one tile
from every leaf that we
find. She cuts the stalks
to the right size and then
weaves them round a
piece of stick which
she balances between
her toes.

She works very quickly
and can make over two
hundred tiles a week.
Each one is worth a
shilling and she either
sells them to our
neighbours or at the
little market in
Mullaleo.

When the tiles are first
put on a roof there are
still small gaps between
the stalks. But as the
palms soak up the rain,
they begin to swell and
the gaps close up.

Dad works for one of the biggest ironmongers in Mombasa, called Doshi Company. They sell cement, tools and fertilizer to builders and farmers. Dad works in the office above the shop. He has to keep a note of everything that is sold and then order more, so that they never run short downstairs.

Dad comes home at six and gets changed. When Mum's away, I cook our evening meal. We usually have ugali, which is a sort of mash, made from maize flour and water. I cook over a wood-fire in the corner of our yard. I have to keep stirring the ugali to stop it sticking to the pan and burning.

When the ugali is ready, I serve it with a sauce. One of my favourite sauces is made of spinach and is called sukuma wiki, which means 'finish the week'. It's called that because we buy spinach when we don't have enough money to buy meat or fish.

In the evenings, Dad earns some extra money by running a coffee stall outside our house. I often help him. The coffee is served in tiny, pottery cups. It's very strong and we never put sugar in it. The customers are mostly our neighbours and they sit on logs and chat away. I like listening to them while I fill their cups and heat up coffee.

Even on a Sunday, Dad has work to do. He goes into the countryside to visit the farmers and buy their coconuts. Here he is selling them to Mr Ali, one of our neighbours, who will take them to Mombasa market in his truck.

The coconuts are worth quite a lot because the white flesh inside can be turned into soap or cooking oil after it's been dried over a fire. Dad always keeps one or two coconuts so we can use them for cooking.

I'm helping Mum make a coconut sauce for lunch. I use a sharp stick to split the shell of the coconut. Then I sit on the mbuzi, which is a special kind of stool with a point on the front which we use to grate the coconut.

I mix the grated coconut with water and put the mixture in a kifumbo. That's a little basket made of woven grass. When you squeeze the basket, the water comes out flavoured by the coconut and is then ready for cooking. This way there aren't any grated bits to get stuck in your teeth.

Dad finishes early on Sunday so we can eat outside under our mango tree where it's nice and cool. Mum's cooked some fish and ugali, as well as my coconut sauce. Unless we have guests we all eat out of the same big bowl. You take a bit of ugali in the fingers of your right hand and dip it into the sauce. Then you pop it into your mouth – delicious!

Mum spends most of the year on our farm in Bomane, where Dad's family still lives. Now that the Christmas holidays are over, it's time for her to return there and we're going with her to visit our relatives.

Bomane is nearly ten miles away. Sometimes we walk there, but this time we're going by taxi, because Mum has so much to carry. The biggest thing of all is her bed. She wants to take it up to her house. Our neighbours are helping to take it apart while we do some last minute jobs.

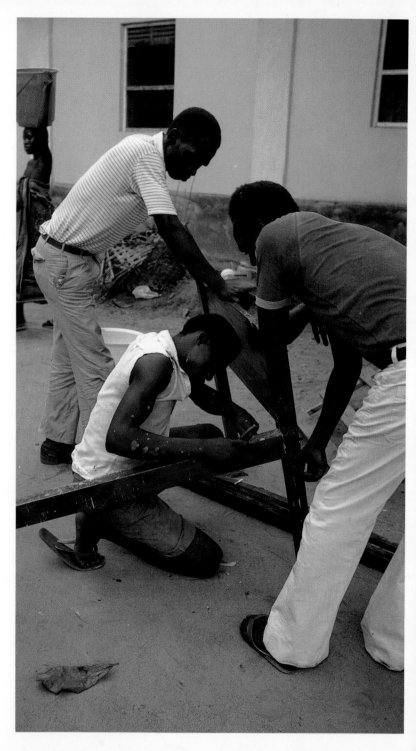

Before we go, Mum takes Rita for a check-up at the medical centre in Mullaleo. It's better equipped than the one in Bomane. The nurse puts Rita on the scales to check that she is growing normally. Afterwards, we have to visit the chemist to buy medicine and then go to the other shops.

There are no proper roads to Bomane and when the taxi finally drops us off we still have a long way to walk. We leave the bed by the track for one of our relatives to come and collect later on. We carry the other luggage between us. Mum has a bagful of shopping on her head. She's bought sugar, salt, fish and meat, all the things you don't find in Bomane. I carry Christopher – it's tiring carrying him uphill.

Uncle Joseph has come down to meet us. He has his own farm at Bomane. He's always telling jokes and it's nice to see him again.

Uncle Joseph is Dad's eldest brother. Altogether, I have six uncles and lots of cousins living in Bomane. Dad can only come to the farm for a month every year, when he has time off work. But when he retires, he'll come back and live with Mum in Bomane.

On Mum's farm, we have three cows, five goats and some chickens. The cows are very thin now because for the last few months there's been no rain to make the grass grow.

One of the good things about Bomane is that we can drink fresh milk. The bad thing is that I have to get the milk myself! I don't like cows and always stand well clear when I'm milking so I won't get my dress dirty. Luckily my cousin isn't busy so he can hold the cow's head to stop her running off.

Looking after the farm is a lot of work for Mum. When it starts to rain, she will have to spend every day in the fields preparing the soil for planting. We grow maize, beans and cashew nuts on our farm and next year Mum wants to try some rice, too. Everyone prefers rice to maize, but it's much harder to grow.

When the cashew nuts are ripe, most of the crop is sold to the government. We always make sure to keep some behind for ourselves though. My cousins spend hours cooking cashew nuts on little bits of hot charcoal. This makes the nuts crunchy – Christopher really likes them.

Between April and June, there's always plenty of
rain where we live, so we usually have a good
harvest. Mum stores the beans and maize for us to
eat later in the year. When she goes to Mombasa
she always takes masses of food.

In Bomane everyone grinds their own maize. My
aunt keeps her grinding stones outside her house.
First she toasts the maize over the fire. Then she
trickles it through the hole on top of the grinding
stones. When she turns the wooden handle, the
maize is crushed between the stones. It's very
slow, of course, but home-ground maize tastes
much better than the kind we buy in Mombasa.

In the evenings, we play games or listen to the grown-ups tell stories. My uncles like to play a game called Kigogo. You can play it with round stones or dried beans. I know the aim is to take the other players' pieces, but I find Kigogo very hard to understand. The men's hands move so fast across the board, dropping beans here and there, that it's difficult to follow.

I like draughts better. We play under the trees opposite our house; I'm playing with my cousin, James. We use bottle-tops for draughts and a piece of wood for the board. James sits on a hollowed tree-trunk, which is normally used for pounding maize into flour. He's very good at draughts and I've never beaten him, but I keep trying!

The new school term is just about to start so we can't stay in Bomane very long. The quickest way of getting home is to follow the footpath. Mum walks back with us in case we lose the way. When we arrive at the river, Mum pays the man to paddle us across in a canoe. It's a very long walk. By the time we reach our house I'm really thirsty.

I'm looking forward to going back to school and I've already bought my exercise books and pencils. It costs Dad over a hundred shillings every term to send me to school and he also has to buy my uniform. Dad says he wants us to have the best education and that's why we go to school in Mombasa.

At our school, we learn arithmetic, geography, hygiene and Swahili, which is the most common language in Kenya. I also speak a bit of English, but I won't study it properly until I move up to secondary school.

I miss Mum an awful lot when she's not here, but I think I like Mombasa better than Bomane. All my best friends live here and I enjoy school, because I know it will help me when I am older. And, besides, Dad works so hard, he needs someone to look after him!